D1362402

BLACK PANTHER

A NATION UNDER OUR FEET: PART 5

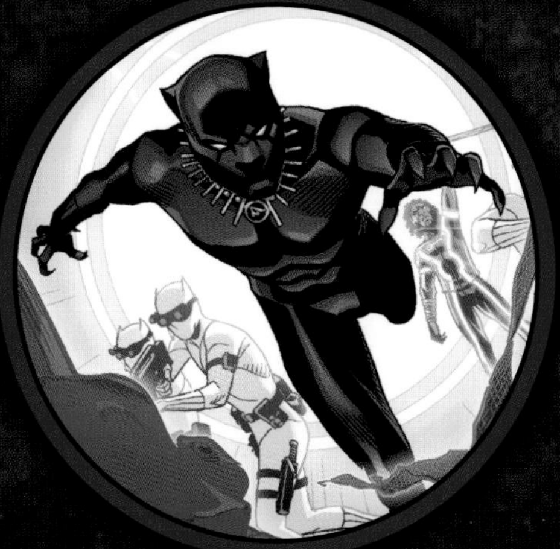

ABDOBOOKS.COM

Reinforced library bound edition published in 2020 by Spotlight, a division of ABDO, PO Box 398166, Minneapolis, Minnesota 55439. Spotlight produces high-quality reinforced library bound editions for schools and libraries. Published by agreement with Marvel Characters, Inc.

Printed in the United States of America, North Mankato, Minnesota.
042019 092019

MARVEL

THIS BOOK CONTAINS RECYCLED MATERIALS

Library of Congress Control Number: 2018965952

Publisher's Cataloging-in-Publication Data

Names: Coates, Ta-Nehisi, author. | Stelfreeze, Brian; Martin, Laura; Sprouse, Chris; Story, Karl, illustrators.
Title: A nation under our feet / writer: Ta-Nehisi Coates; art: Brian Stelfreeze ; Laura Martin ; Chris Sprouse ; Karl Story.
Description: Minneapolis, Minnesota : Spotlight, 2020 | Series: Black Panther
Summary: With a dramatic upheaval in Wakanda on the horizon, T'Challa knows his kingdom needs to change to survive, but he struggles to find balance in his roles as king and the Black Panther.
Identifiers: ISBN 9781532143519 (pt. 1 ; lib. bdg.) | ISBN 9781532143526 (pt. 2 ; lib. bdg.) | ISBN 9781532143533 (pt. 3 ; lib. bdg.) | ISBN 9781532143540 (pt. 4 ; lib. bdg.) | ISBN 9781532143557 (pt. 5 ; lib. bdg.) | ISBN 9781532143564 (pt. 6 ; lib. bdg.)
Subjects: LCSH: Black Panther (Fictitious character)--Juvenile fiction. | Superheroes--Juvenile fiction. | Kings and rulers--Juvenile fiction. | Graphic novels--Juvenile fiction. | T'Challa, of Wakanda (Fictitious character)--Juvenile fiction.
Classification: DDC 741.5--dc23

ABDO
Spotlight

A Division of ABDO
abdobooks.com

BLACK PANTHER

TETU AND **ZENZI**, LEADERS OF THE INSURGENT GROUP KNOWN AS **THE PEOPLE**, HAVE STOKED THE GROWING FEELINGS OF DISSENT AMONG THE CITIZENS OF WAKANDA. THEY COURTED THE ASSISTANCE OF FORMER DORA MILAJE **AYO** AND **ANEKA**, NOW KNOWN AS **THE MIDNIGHT ANGELS**, TO SUPPPORT THEIR REBELLION.

AFTER AYO AND ANEKA DECLINED, TETU TURNED TO **EZEKIEL STANE**, WEAPONEER AND BIOTECHNOLOGY EXPERT, TO RAISE THE STAKES OF THEIR WAR: REPULSOR-TECH SUICIDE BOMBERS ATTACKED A CITY SQUARE, KILLING MANY INNOCENTS AND SEVERELY INJURING QUEEN-MOTHER **RAMONDA**.

THE SITUATION NOW HAS KING **T'CHALLA'S** FULL ATTENTION, AS HE PUTS ASIDE A VERY PERSONAL PROJECT: REVIVING HIS SISTER **SHURI** FROM LIVING DEATH. UNBEKNOWNST TO HIM, SHURI'S MIND TRAVELS THE DJALIA, A PLANE OF WAKANDA'S COLLECTIVE PAST, PRESENT, AND FUTURE. SHE IS GUIDED BY A GRIOT SPIRIT WHO HAS TAKEN THE VISUAL FORM OF RAMONDA.

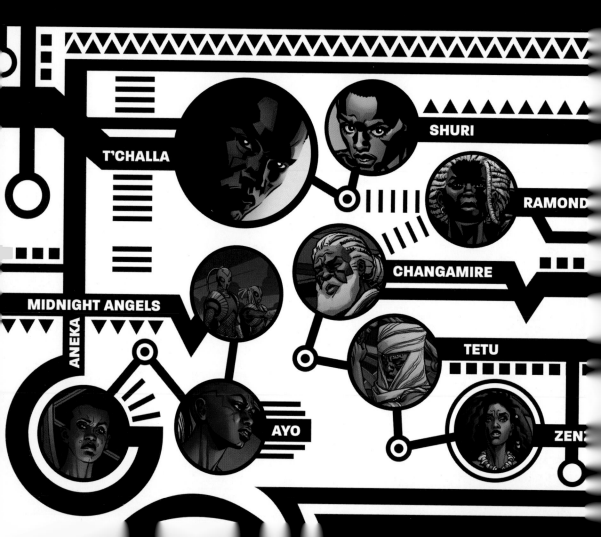

T'CHALLA

SHURI

RAMOND

CHANGAMIRE

MIDNIGHT ANGELS

ANEKA

AYO

TETU

ZEN

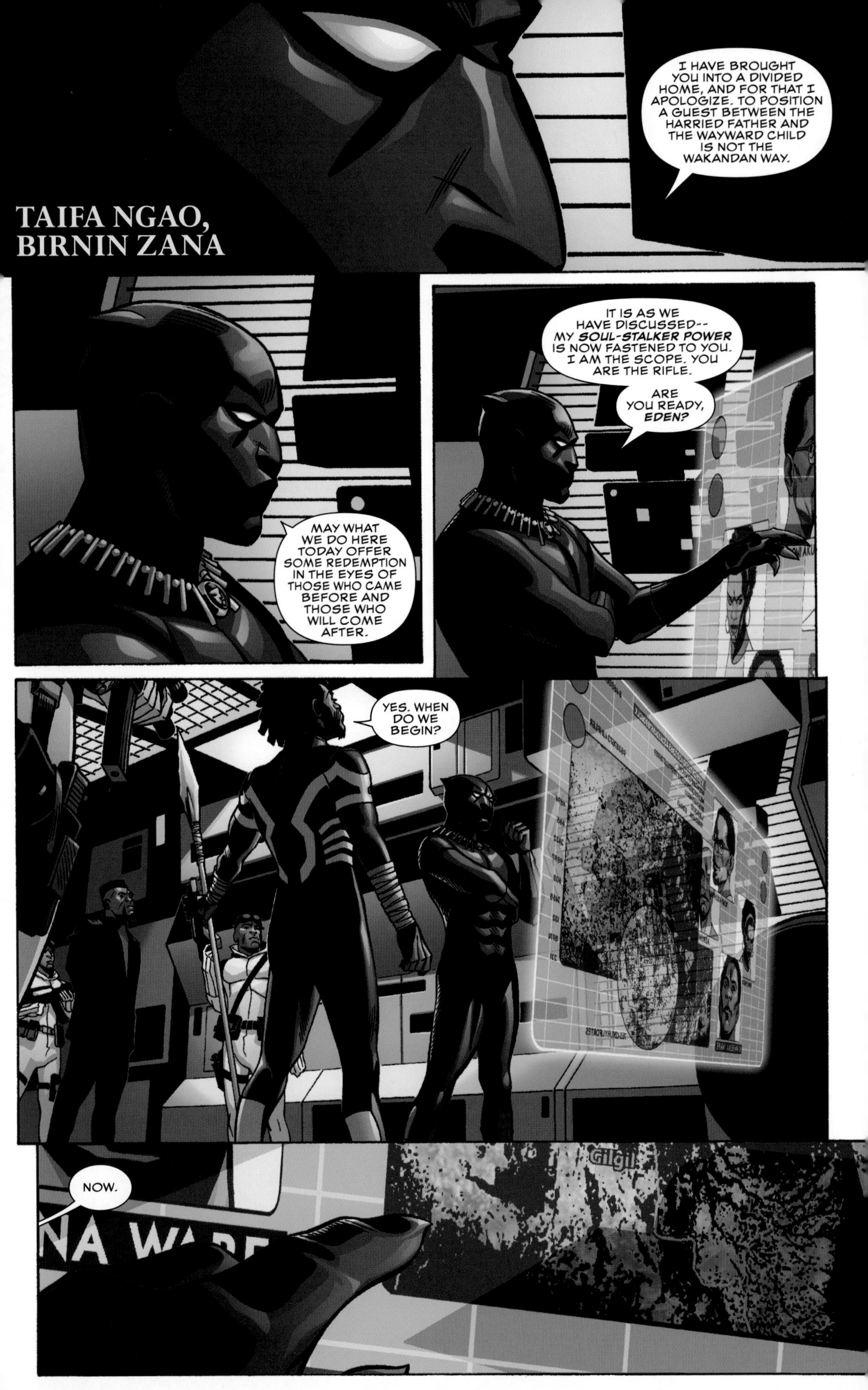
I HAVE BROUGHT YOU INTO A DIVIDED HOME, AND FOR THAT I APOLOGIZE. TO POSITION A GUEST BETWEEN THE HARRIED FATHER AND THE WAYWARD CHILD IS NOT THE WAKANDAN WAY.
TAIFA NGAO, BIRNIN ZANA
MAY WHAT WE DO HERE TODAY OFFER SOME REDEMPTION IN THE EYES OF THOSE WHO CAME BEFORE AND THOSE WHO WILL COME AFTER.
IT IS AS WE HAVE DISCUSSED-- MY SOUL-STALKER POWER IS NOW FASTENED TO YOU. I AM THE SCOPE. YOU ARE THE RIFLE.
ARE YOU READY, EDEN?
YES. WHEN DO WE BEGIN?
NOW.
Gilgil

writer **TA-NEHISI COATES**

penciler **CHRIS SPROUSE** inker **KARL STORY**

color artist **LAURA MARTIN**

A NATIC

UNDER OUR

letterer **VC's JOE SABINO** design **MANNY MEDEROS**
logo by **RIAN HUGHES** cover by **BRIAN STELFREEZE**
& **LAURA MARTIN** variant covers by **JOHN CASSADAY**
& **PAUL MOUNTS, GREG HILDEBRANDT, KABAM**
with **GABRIEL FRIZZERA, SARA PICHELLI & JASON KEITH,**
ESAD RIBIC, JIM STERANKO
assistant editor **CHRIS ROBINSON**
editor **WIL MOSS**
executive editor **TOM BREVOORT**

editor in chief **AXEL ALONSO** chief creative officer **JOE QUESADA** publisher **DAN BUCKLEY** executive producer **ALAN FINE**

BLACK PANTHER

created by
STAN LEE &
JACK KIRBY

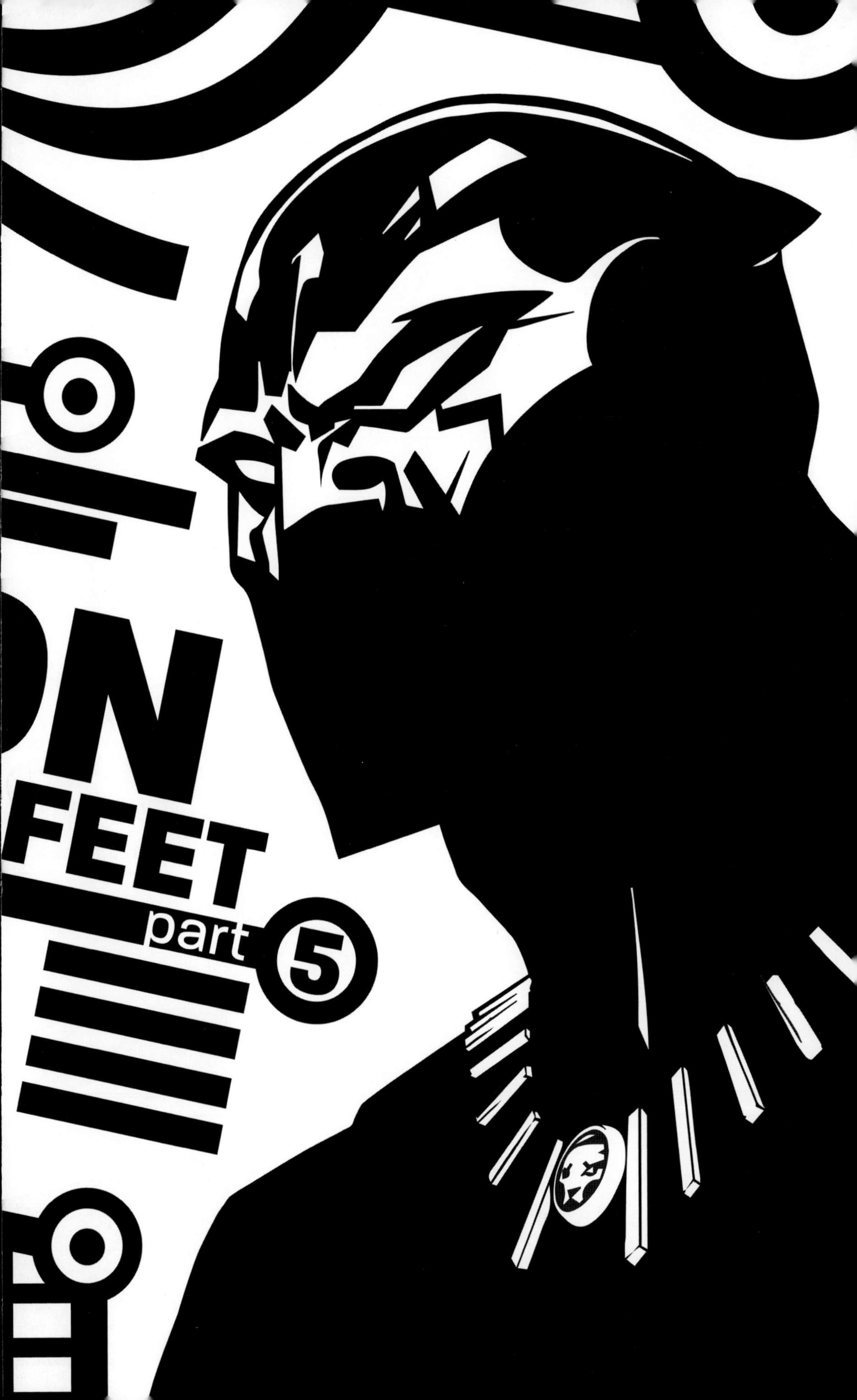
FEET
part 5

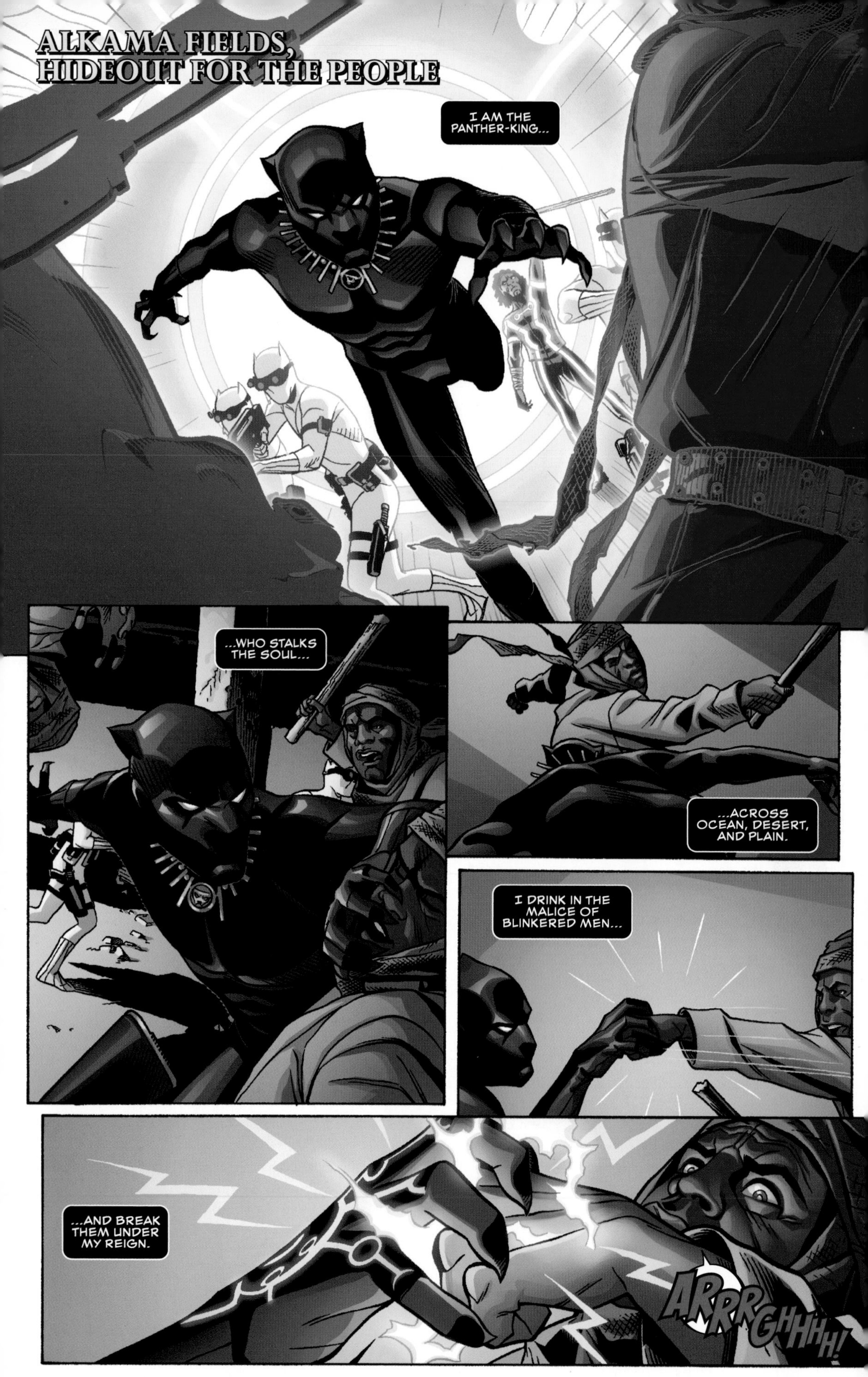

ALKAMA FIELDS, HIDEOUT FOR THE PEOPLE
I AM THE PANTHER-KING...
...WHO STALKS THE SOUL...
...ACROSS OCEAN, DESERT, AND PLAIN.
I DRINK IN THE MALICE OF BLINKERED MEN...
...AND BREAK THEM UNDER MY REIGN.
ARRRGHHHH!

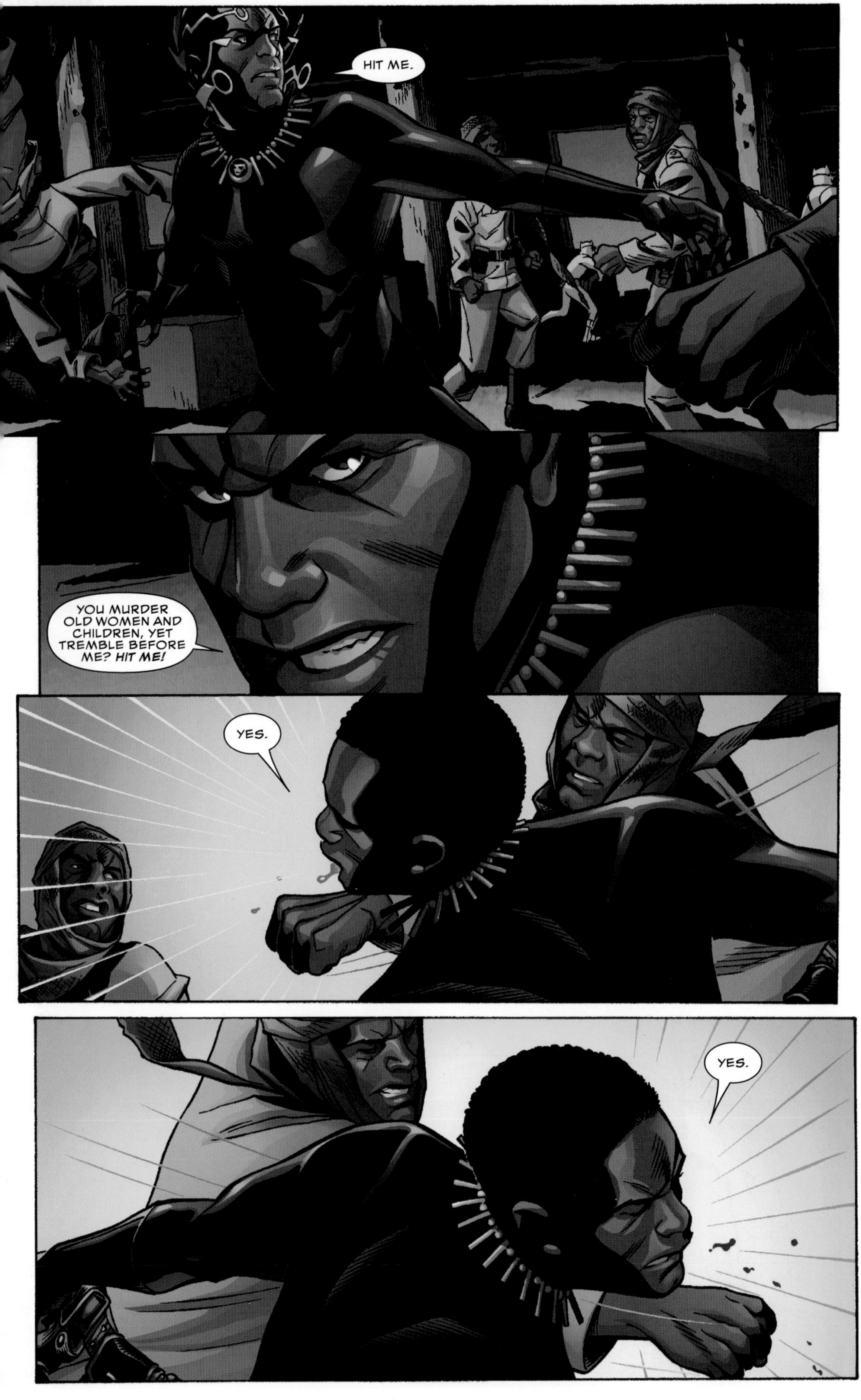
HIT ME.
YOU MURDER OLD WOMEN AND CHILDREN, YET TREMBLE BEFORE ME? *HIT ME!*
YES.
YES.

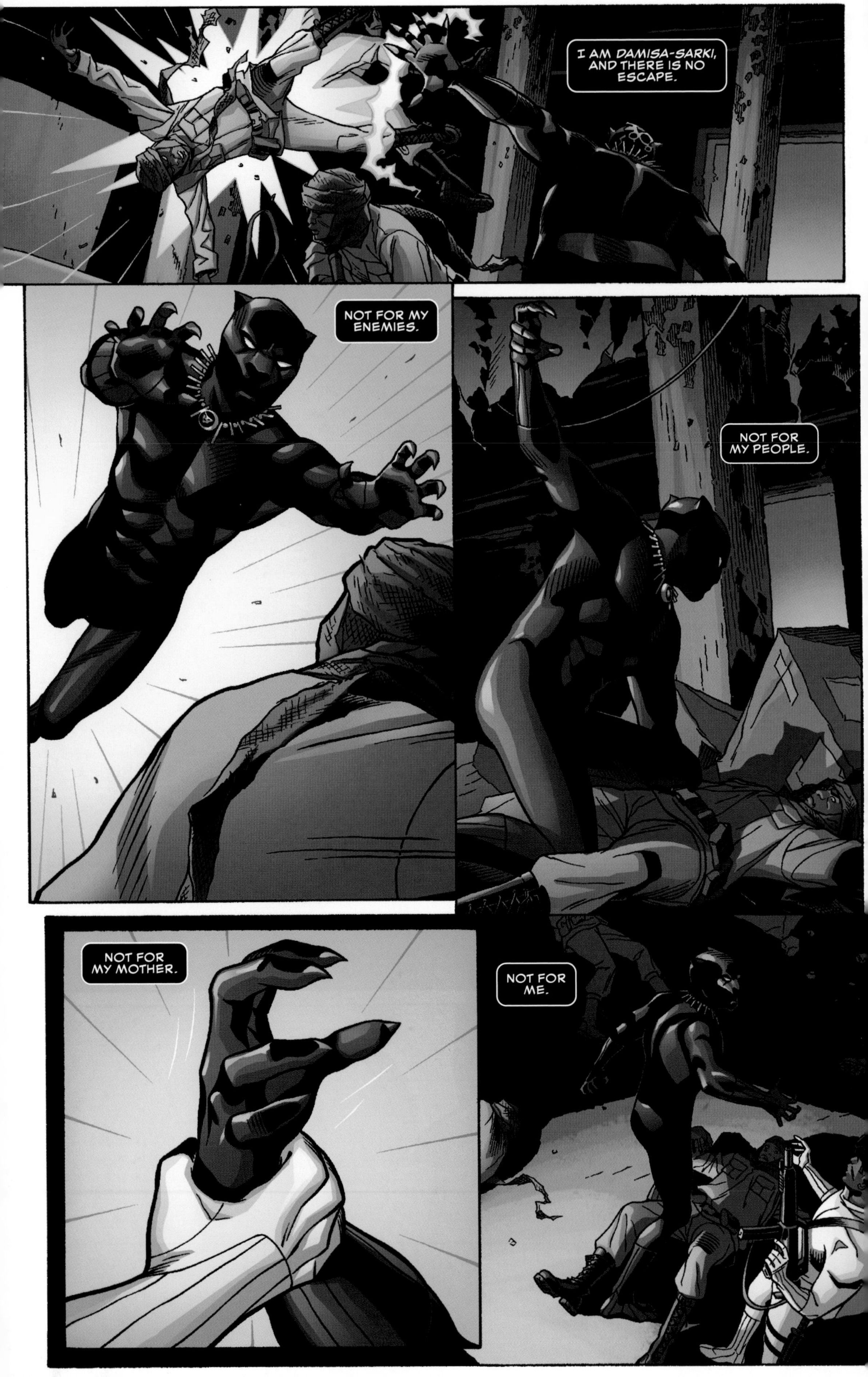
I AM DAMISA-SARKI, AND THERE IS NO ESCAPE.
NOT FOR MY ENEMIES.
NOT FOR MY PEOPLE.
NOT FOR MY MOTHER.
NOT FOR ME.

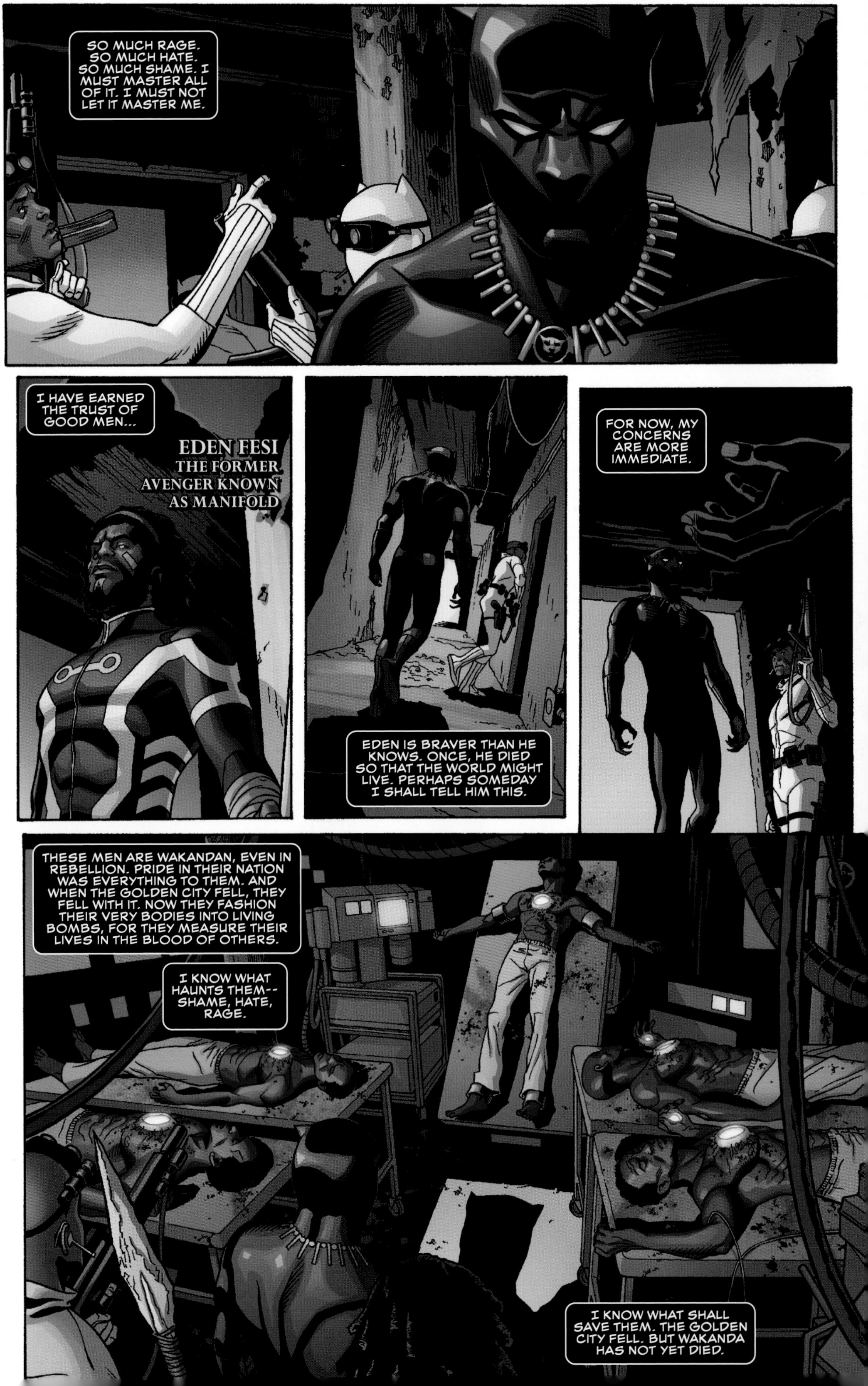
SO MUCH RAGE. SO MUCH HATE. SO MUCH SHAME. I MUST MASTER ALL OF IT. I MUST NOT LET IT MASTER ME.
I HAVE EARNED THE TRUST OF GOOD MEN...
EDEN FESI THE FORMER AVENGER KNOWN AS MANIFOLD
EDEN IS BRAVER THAN HE KNOWS. ONCE, HE DIED SO THAT THE WORLD MIGHT LIVE. PERHAPS SOMEDAY I SHALL TELL HIM THIS.
FOR NOW, MY CONCERNS ARE MORE IMMEDIATE.
THESE MEN ARE WAKANDAN, EVEN IN REBELLION. PRIDE IN THEIR NATION WAS EVERYTHING TO THEM. AND WHEN THE GOLDEN CITY FELL, THEY FELL WITH IT. NOW THEY FASHION THEIR VERY BODIES INTO LIVING BOMBS, FOR THEY MEASURE THEIR LIVES IN THE BLOOD OF OTHERS.
I KNOW WHAT HAUNTS THEM-- SHAME, HATE, RAGE.
I KNOW WHAT SHALL SAVE THEM. THE GOLDEN CITY FELL. BUT WAKANDA HAS NOT YET DIED.

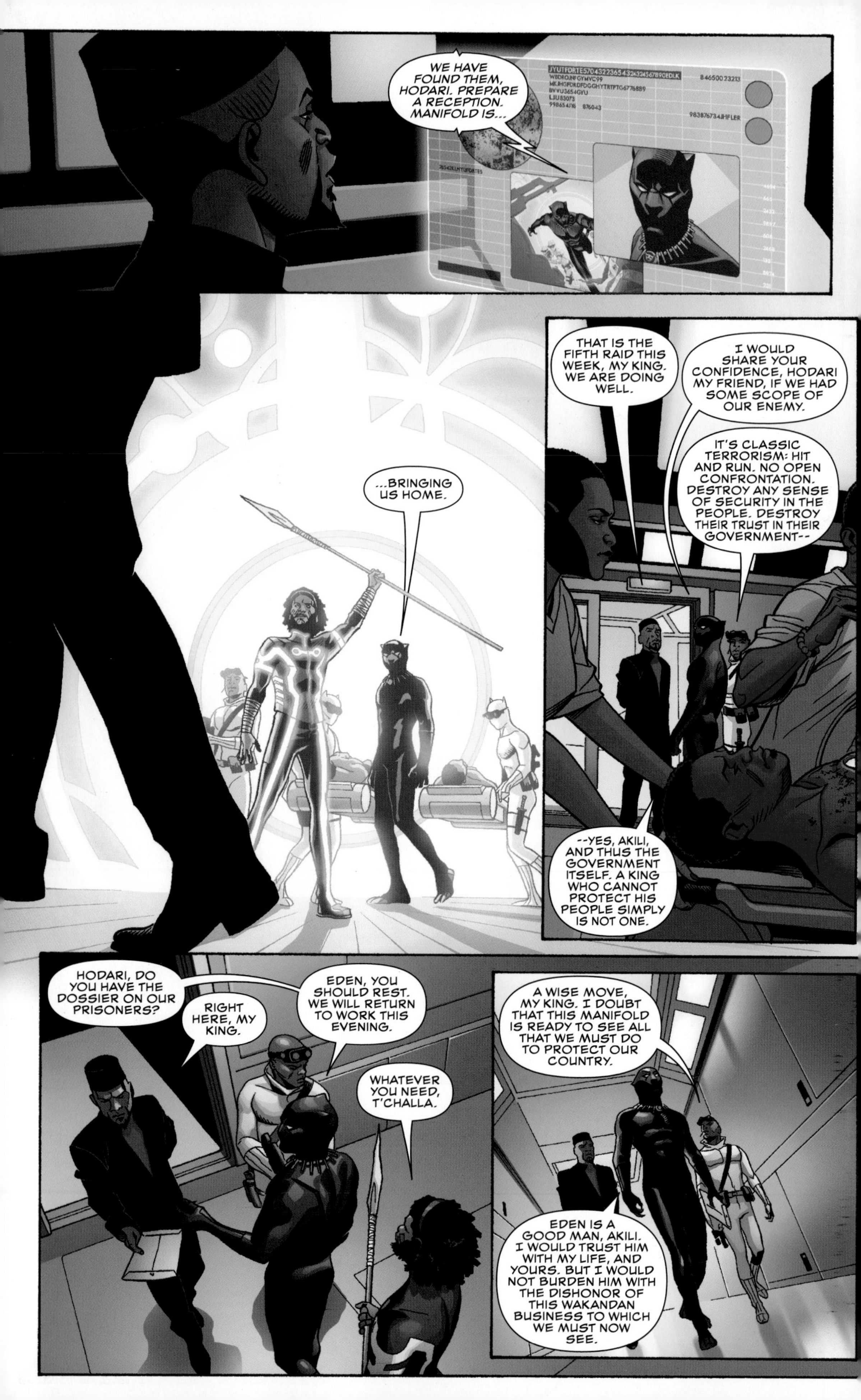
WE HAVE FOUND THEM, HODARI. PREPARE A RECEPTION. MANIFOLD IS...
...BRINGING US HOME.
THAT IS THE FIFTH RAID THIS WEEK, MY KING. WE ARE DOING WELL.
I WOULD SHARE YOUR CONFIDENCE, HODARI MY FRIEND, IF WE HAD SOME SCOPE OF OUR ENEMY.
IT'S CLASSIC TERRORISM: HIT AND RUN. NO OPEN CONFRONTATION. DESTROY ANY SENSE OF SECURITY IN THE PEOPLE. DESTROY THEIR TRUST IN THEIR GOVERNMENT--
--YES, AKILI, AND THUS THE GOVERNMENT ITSELF. A KING WHO CANNOT PROTECT HIS PEOPLE SIMPLY IS NOT ONE.
HODARI, DO YOU HAVE THE DOSSIER ON OUR PRISONERS?
RIGHT HERE, MY KING.
EDEN, YOU SHOULD REST. WE WILL RETURN TO WORK THIS EVENING.
WHATEVER YOU NEED, T'CHALLA.
A WISE MOVE, MY KING. I DOUBT THAT THIS MANIFOLD IS READY TO SEE ALL THAT WE MUST DO TO PROTECT OUR COUNTRY.
EDEN IS A GOOD MAN, AKILI. I WOULD TRUST HIM WITH MY LIFE, AND YOURS. BUT I WOULD NOT BURDEN HIM WITH THE DISHONOR OF THIS WAKANDAN BUSINESS TO WHICH WE MUST NOW SEE.

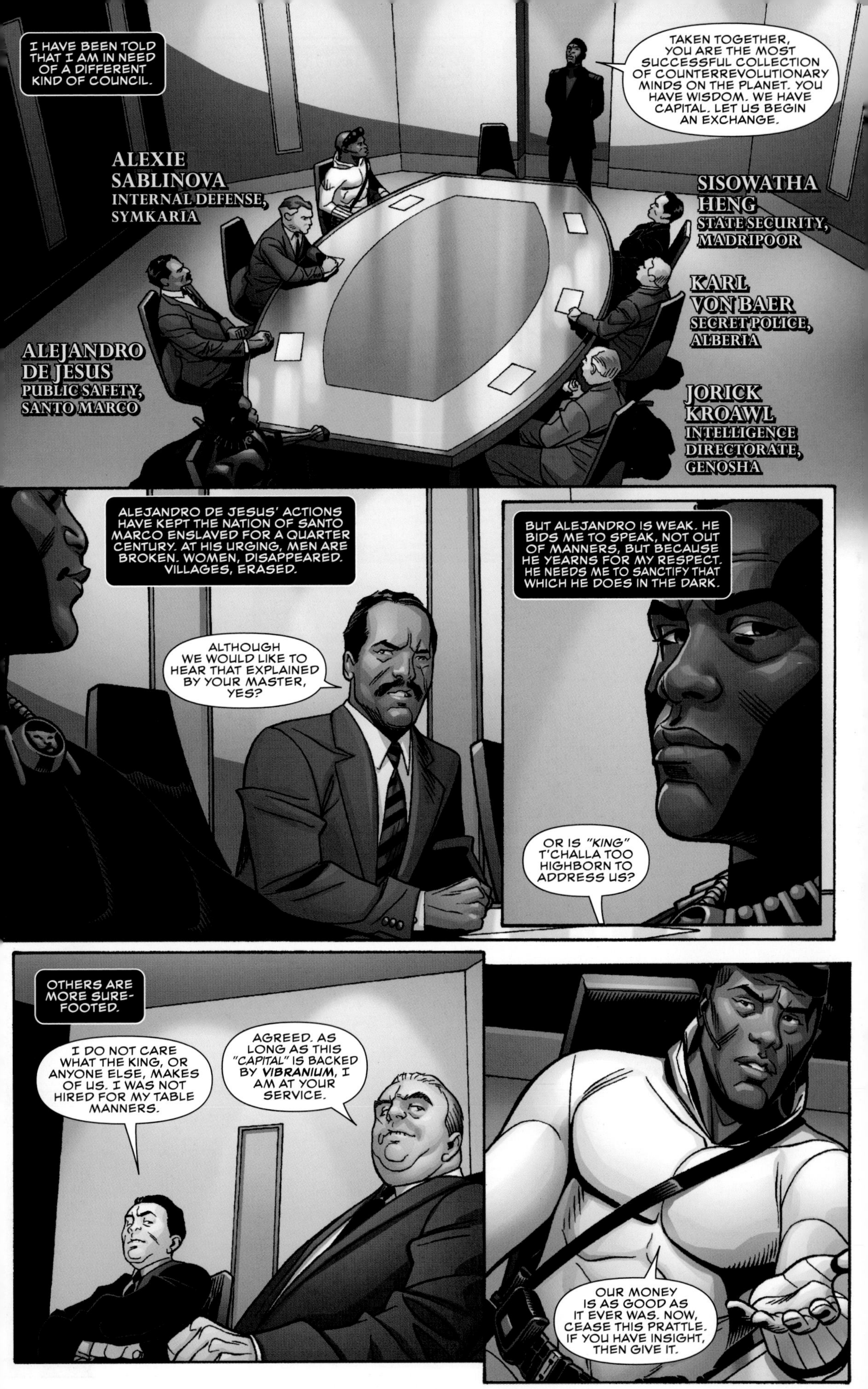

I HAVE BEEN TOLD THAT I AM IN NEED OF A DIFFERENT KIND OF COUNCIL.
TAKEN TOGETHER, YOU ARE THE MOST SUCCESSFUL COLLECTION OF COUNTERREVOLUTIONARY MINDS ON THE PLANET. YOU HAVE WISDOM. WE HAVE CAPITAL. LET US BEGIN AN EXCHANGE.
ALEXIE SABLINOVA INTERNAL DEFENSE, SYMKARIA
SISOWATHA HENG STATE SECURITY, MADRIPOOR
KARL VON BAER SECRET POLICE, ALBERIA
ALEJANDRO DE JESUS PUBLIC SAFETY, SANTO MARCO
JORICK KROAWL INTELLIGENCE DIRECTORATE, GENOSHA
ALEJANDRO DE JESUS' ACTIONS HAVE KEPT THE NATION OF SANTO MARCO ENSLAVED FOR A QUARTER CENTURY. AT HIS URGING, MEN ARE BROKEN. WOMEN, DISAPPEARED. VILLAGES, ERASED.
ALTHOUGH WE WOULD LIKE TO HEAR THAT EXPLAINED BY YOUR MASTER, YES?
BUT ALEJANDRO IS WEAK. HE BIDS ME TO SPEAK, NOT OUT OF MANNERS, BUT BECAUSE HE YEARNS FOR MY RESPECT. HE NEEDS ME TO SANCTIFY THAT WHICH HE DOES IN THE DARK.
OR IS "KING" T'CHALLA TOO HIGHBORN TO ADDRESS US?
OTHERS ARE MORE SURE-FOOTED.
I DO NOT CARE WHAT THE KING, OR ANYONE ELSE, MAKES OF US. I WAS NOT HIRED FOR MY TABLE MANNERS.
AGREED. AS LONG AS THIS "CAPITAL" IS BACKED BY VIBRANIUM, I AM AT YOUR SERVICE.
OUR MONEY IS AS GOOD AS IT EVER WAS. NOW, CEASE THIS PRATTLE. IF YOU HAVE INSIGHT, THEN GIVE IT.

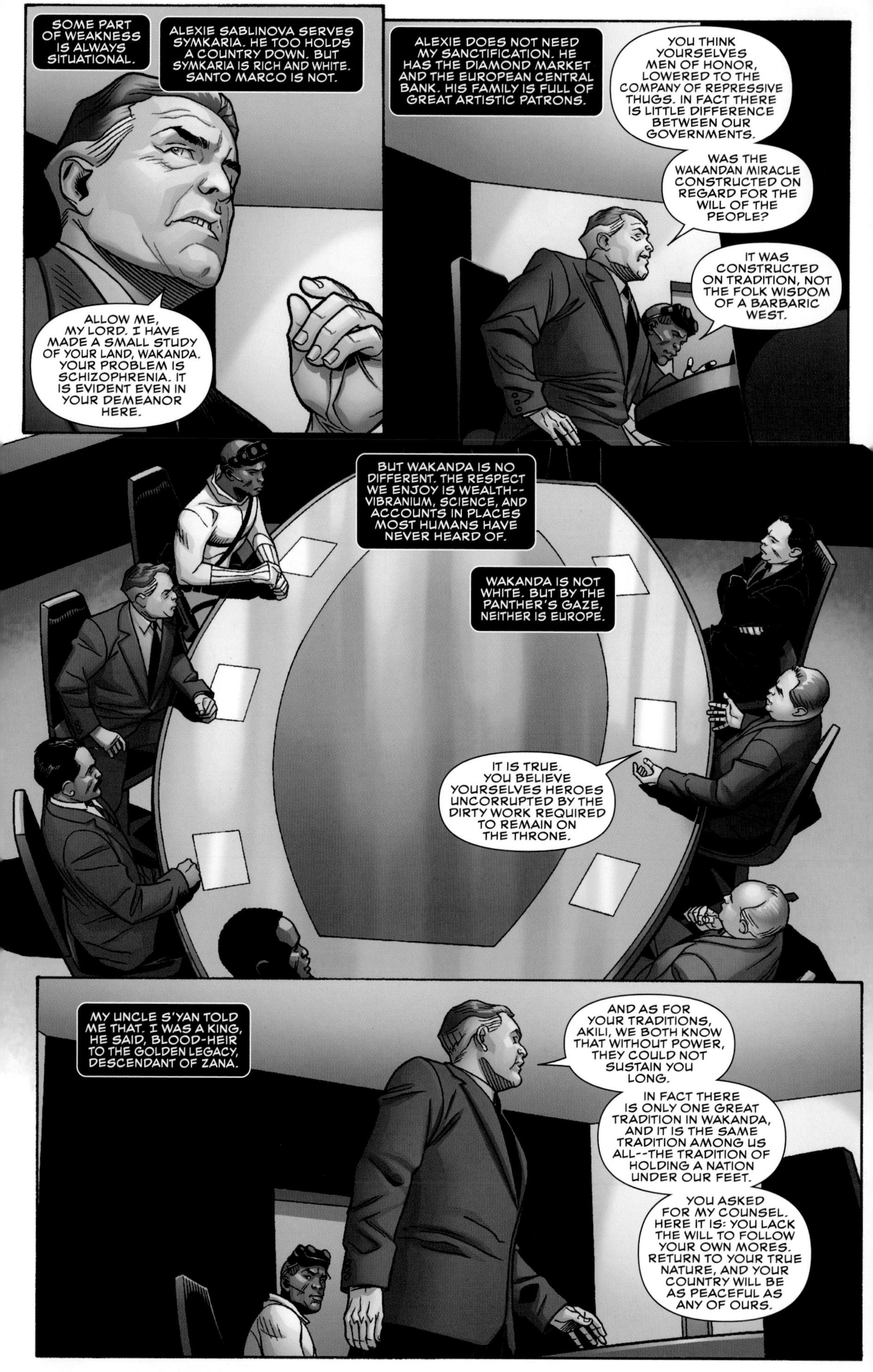
SOME PART OF WEAKNESS IS ALWAYS SITUATIONAL.
ALEXIE SABLINOVA SERVES SYMKARIA. HE TOO HOLDS A COUNTRY DOWN. BUT SYMKARIA IS RICH AND WHITE. SANTO MARCO IS NOT.
ALLOW ME, MY LORD. I HAVE MADE A SMALL STUDY OF YOUR LAND, WAKANDA. YOUR PROBLEM IS SCHIZOPHRENIA. IT IS EVIDENT EVEN IN YOUR DEMEANOR HERE.
ALEXIE DOES NOT NEED MY SANCTIFICATION. HE HAS THE DIAMOND MARKET AND THE EUROPEAN CENTRAL BANK. HIS FAMILY IS FULL OF GREAT ARTISTIC PATRONS.
YOU THINK YOURSELVES MEN OF HONOR, LOWERED TO THE COMPANY OF REPRESSIVE THUGS. IN FACT THERE IS LITTLE DIFFERENCE BETWEEN OUR GOVERNMENTS.
WAS THE WAKANDAN MIRACLE CONSTRUCTED ON REGARD FOR THE WILL OF THE PEOPLE?
IT WAS CONSTRUCTED ON TRADITION, NOT THE FOLK WISDOM OF A BARBARIC WEST.
BUT WAKANDA IS NO DIFFERENT. THE RESPECT WE ENJOY IS WEALTH--VIBRANIUM, SCIENCE, AND ACCOUNTS IN PLACES MOST HUMANS HAVE NEVER HEARD OF.
WAKANDA IS NOT WHITE. BUT BY THE PANTHER'S GAZE, NEITHER IS EUROPE.
IT IS TRUE. YOU BELIEVE YOURSELVES HEROES UNCORRUPTED BY THE DIRTY WORK REQUIRED TO REMAIN ON THE THRONE.
MY UNCLE S'YAN TOLD ME THAT. I WAS A KING, HE SAID, BLOOD-HEIR TO THE GOLDEN LEGACY, DESCENDANT OF ZANA.
AND AS FOR YOUR TRADITIONS, AKILI, WE BOTH KNOW THAT WITHOUT POWER, THEY COULD NOT SUSTAIN YOU LONG.
IN FACT THERE IS ONLY ONE GREAT TRADITION IN WAKANDA, AND IT IS THE SAME TRADITION AMONG US ALL--THE TRADITION OF HOLDING A NATION UNDER OUR FEET.
YOU ASKED FOR MY COUNSEL. HERE IT IS: YOU LACK THE WILL TO FOLLOW YOUR OWN MORES. RETURN TO YOUR TRUE NATURE, AND YOUR COUNTRY WILL BE AS PEACEFUL AS ANY OF OURS.

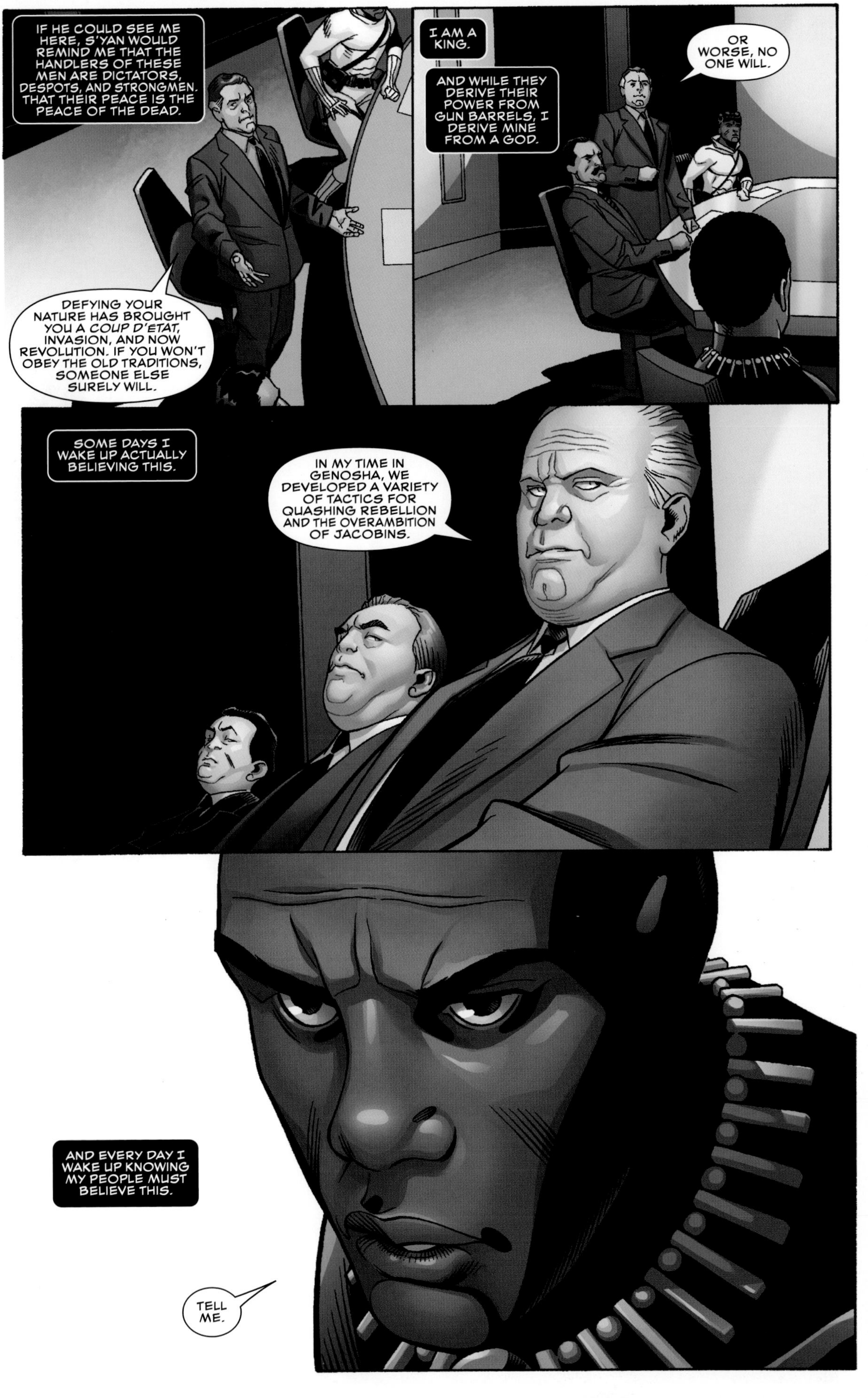
IF HE COULD SEE ME HERE, S'YAN WOULD REMIND ME THAT THE HANDLERS OF THESE MEN ARE DICTATORS, DESPOTS, AND STRONGMEN. THAT THEIR PEACE IS THE PEACE OF THE DEAD.
DEFYING YOUR NATURE HAS BROUGHT YOU A *COUP D'ETAT*, INVASION, AND NOW REVOLUTION. IF YOU WON'T OBEY THE OLD TRADITIONS, SOMEONE ELSE SURELY WILL.
I AM A KING.
AND WHILE THEY DERIVE THEIR POWER FROM GUN BARRELS, I DERIVE MINE FROM A GOD.
OR WORSE, NO ONE WILL.
SOME DAYS I WAKE UP ACTUALLY BELIEVING THIS.
IN MY TIME IN GENOSHA, WE DEVELOPED A VARIETY OF TACTICS FOR QUASHING REBELLION AND THE OVERAMBITION OF JACOBINS.
AND EVERY DAY I WAKE UP KNOWING MY PEOPLE MUST BELIEVE THIS.
TELL ME.

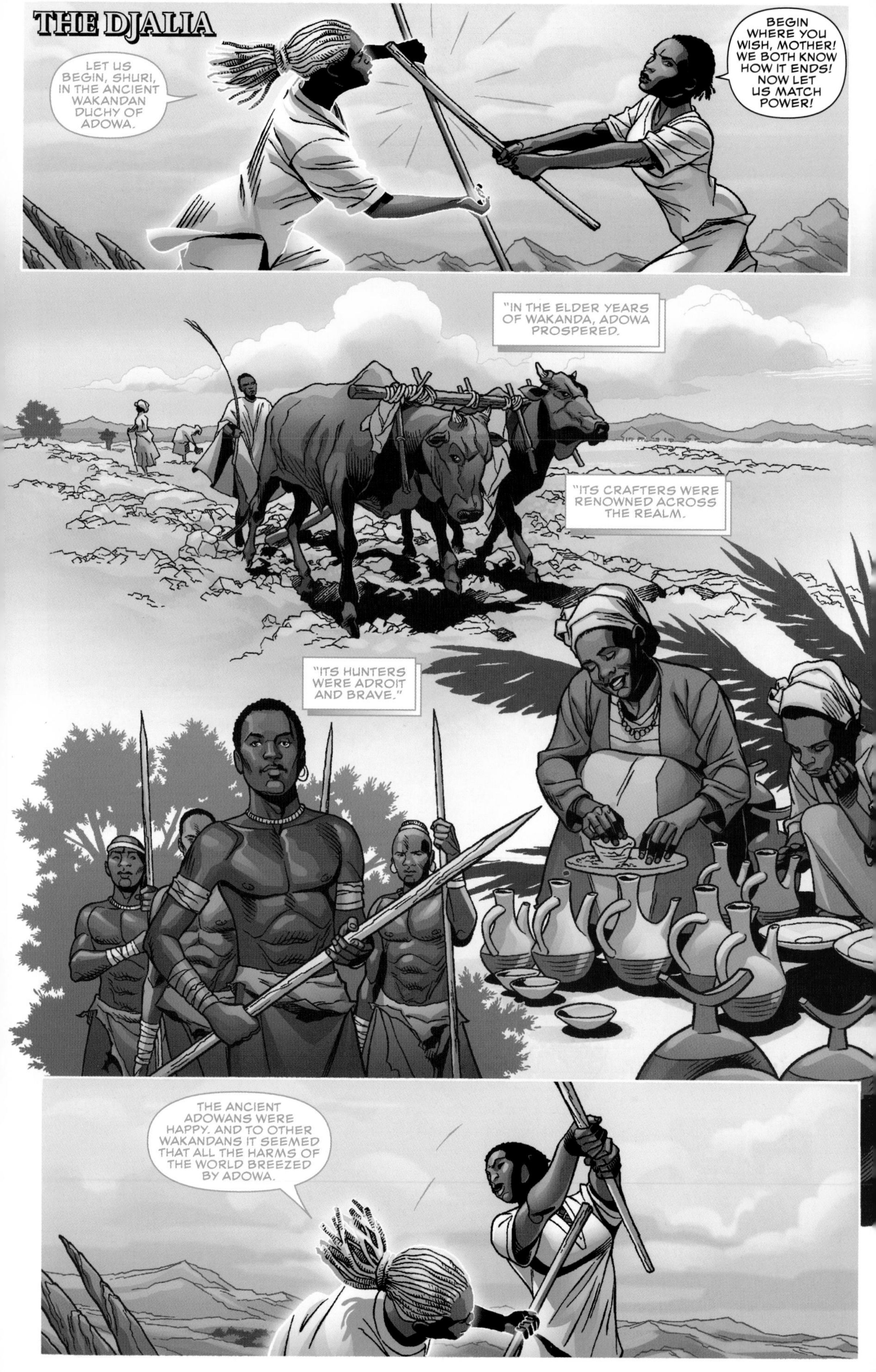
THE DJALIA
LET US BEGIN, SHURI, IN THE ANCIENT WAKANDAN DUCHY OF ADOWA.
BEGIN WHERE YOU WISH, MOTHER! WE BOTH KNOW HOW IT ENDS! NOW LET US MATCH POWER!
"IN THE ELDER YEARS OF WAKANDA, ADOWA PROSPERED.
"ITS CRAFTERS WERE RENOWNED ACROSS THE REALM.
"ITS HUNTERS WERE ADROIT AND BRAVE."
THE ANCIENT ADOWANS WERE HAPPY. AND TO OTHER WAKANDANS IT SEEMED THAT ALL THE HARMS OF THE WORLD BREEZED BY ADOWA.

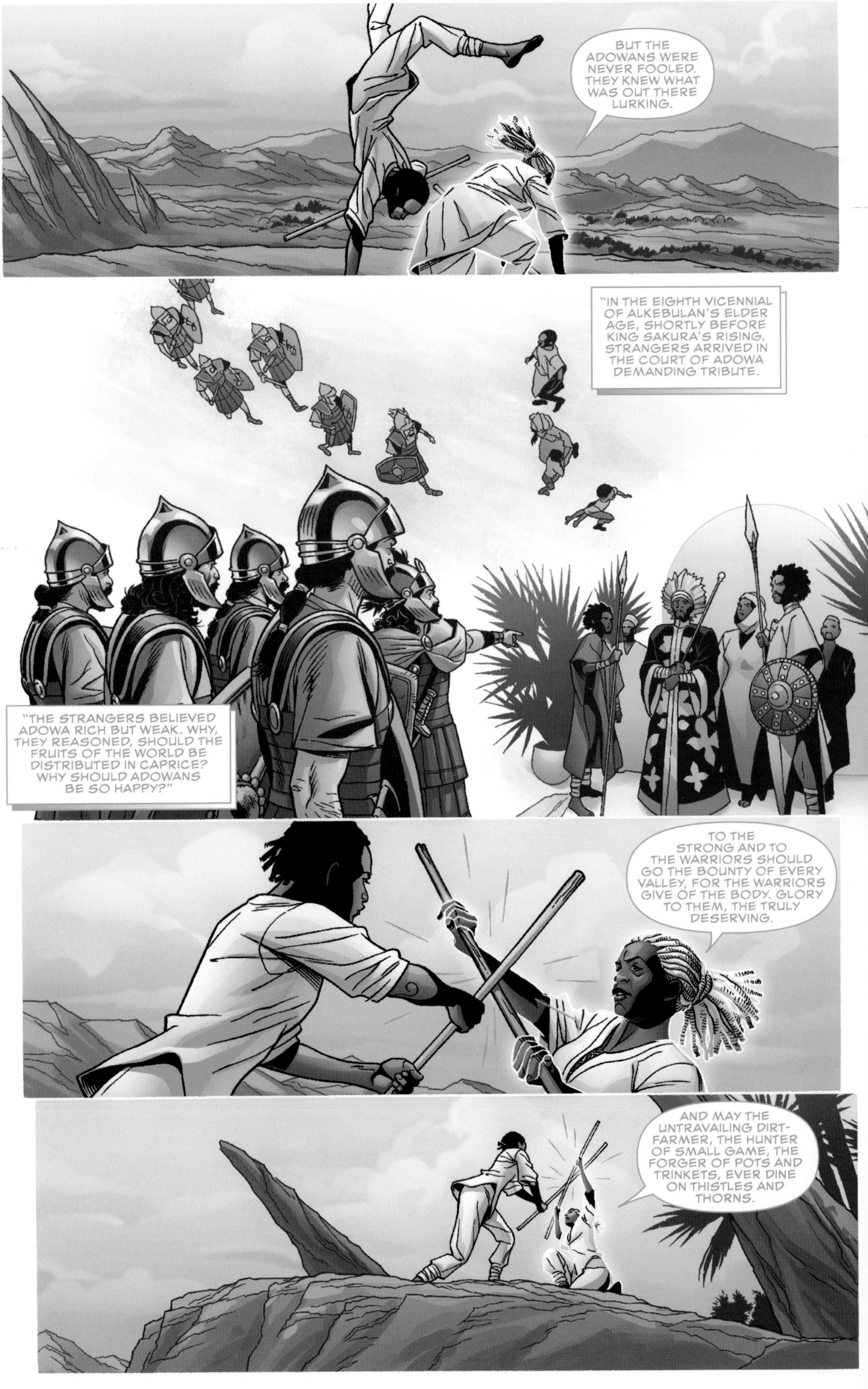

BUT THE ADOWANS WERE NEVER FOOLED. THEY KNEW WHAT WAS OUT THERE LURKING.
"IN THE EIGHTH VICENNIAL OF ALKEBULAN'S ELDER AGE, SHORTLY BEFORE KING SAKURA'S RISING, STRANGERS ARRIVED IN THE COURT OF ADOWA DEMANDING TRIBUTE.
"THE STRANGERS BELIEVED ADOWA RICH BUT WEAK. WHY, THEY REASONED, SHOULD THE FRUITS OF THE WORLD BE DISTRIBUTED IN CAPRICE? WHY SHOULD ADOWANS BE SO HAPPY?"
TO THE STRONG AND TO THE WARRIORS SHOULD GO THE BOUNTY OF EVERY VALLEY, FOR THE WARRIORS GIVE OF THE BODY. GLORY TO THEM, THE TRULY DESERVING.
AND MAY THE UNTRAVAILING DIRT-FARMER, THE HUNTER OF SMALL GAME, THE FORGER OF POTS AND TRINKETS, EVER DINE ON THISTLES AND THORNS.

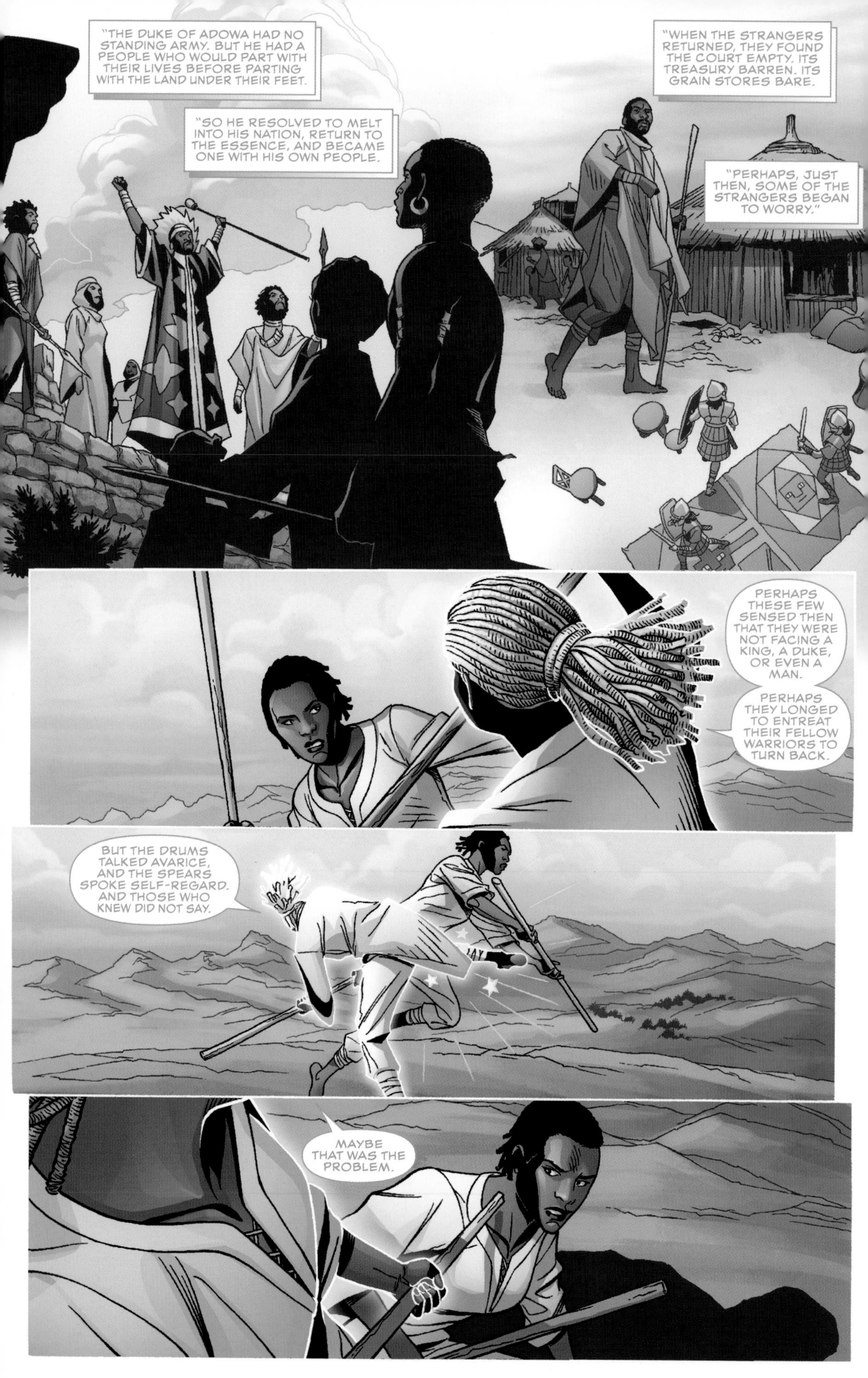
"THE DUKE OF ADOWA HAD NO STANDING ARMY. BUT HE HAD A PEOPLE WHO WOULD PART WITH THEIR LIVES BEFORE PARTING WITH THE LAND UNDER THEIR FEET.
"SO HE RESOLVED TO MELT INTO HIS NATION, RETURN TO THE ESSENCE, AND BECAME ONE WITH HIS OWN PEOPLE.
"WHEN THE STRANGERS RETURNED, THEY FOUND THE COURT EMPTY. ITS TREASURY BARREN. ITS GRAIN STORES BARE.
"PERHAPS, JUST THEN, SOME OF THE STRANGERS BEGAN TO WORRY."
PERHAPS THESE FEW SENSED THEN THAT THEY WERE NOT FACING A KING, A DUKE, OR EVEN A MAN.
PERHAPS THEY LONGED TO ENTREAT THEIR FELLOW WARRIORS TO TURN BACK.
BUT THE DRUMS TALKED AVARICE, AND THE SPEARS SPOKE SELF-REGARD. AND THOSE WHO KNEW DID NOT SAY.
MAYBE THAT WAS THE PROBLEM.

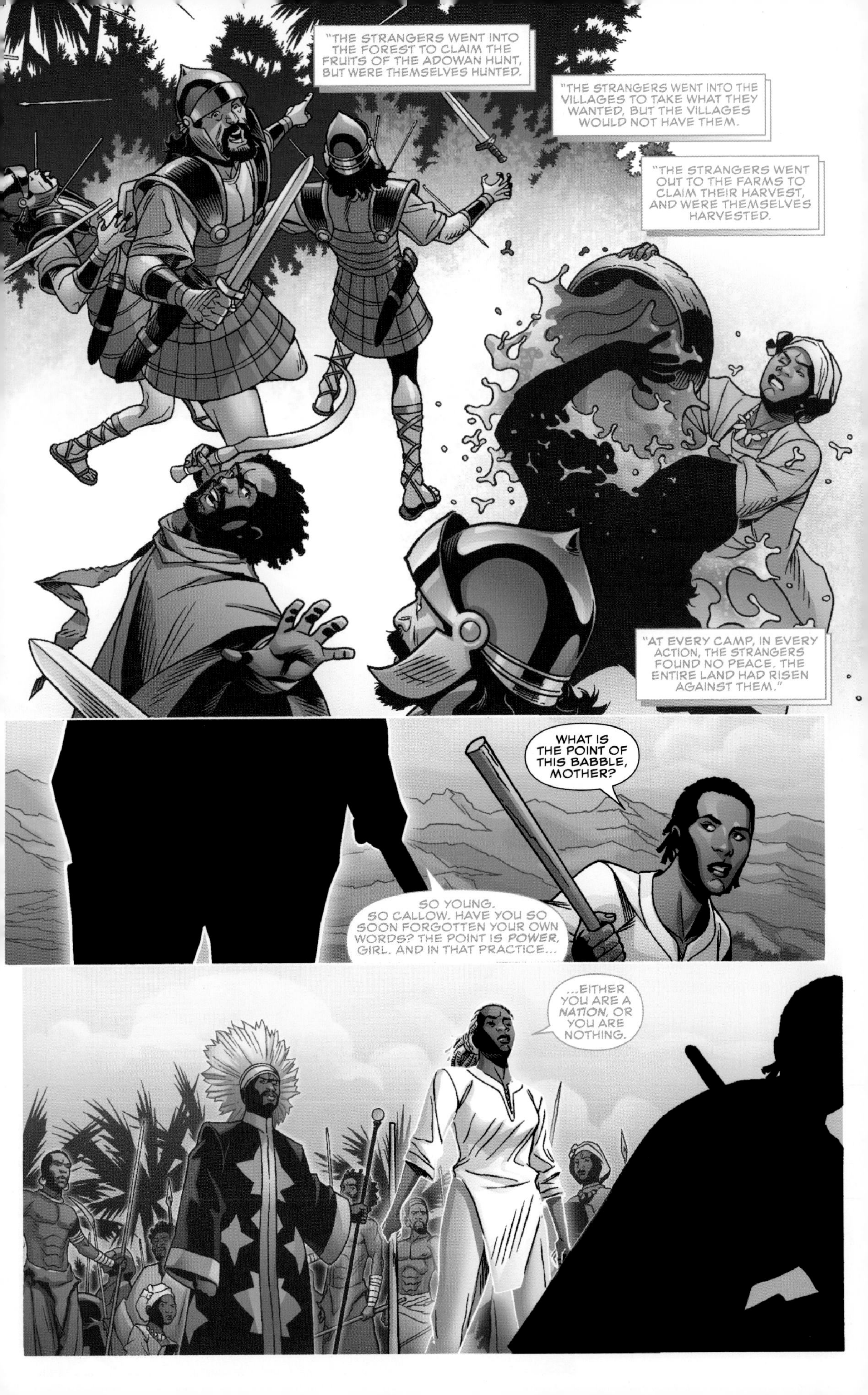
"THE STRANGERS WENT INTO THE FOREST TO CLAIM THE FRUITS OF THE ADOWAN HUNT, BUT WERE THEMSELVES HUNTED.
"THE STRANGERS WENT INTO THE VILLAGES TO TAKE WHAT THEY WANTED, BUT THE VILLAGES WOULD NOT HAVE THEM.
"THE STRANGERS WENT OUT TO THE FARMS TO CLAIM THEIR HARVEST, AND WERE THEMSELVES HARVESTED.
"AT EVERY CAMP, IN EVERY ACTION, THE STRANGERS FOUND NO PEACE. THE ENTIRE LAND HAD RISEN AGAINST THEM."
WHAT IS THE POINT OF THIS BABBLE, MOTHER?
SO YOUNG. SO CALLOW. HAVE YOU SO SOON FORGOTTEN YOUR OWN WORDS? THE POINT IS *POWER*, GIRL. AND IN THAT PRACTICE...
...EITHER YOU ARE A *NATION*, OR YOU ARE NOTHING.

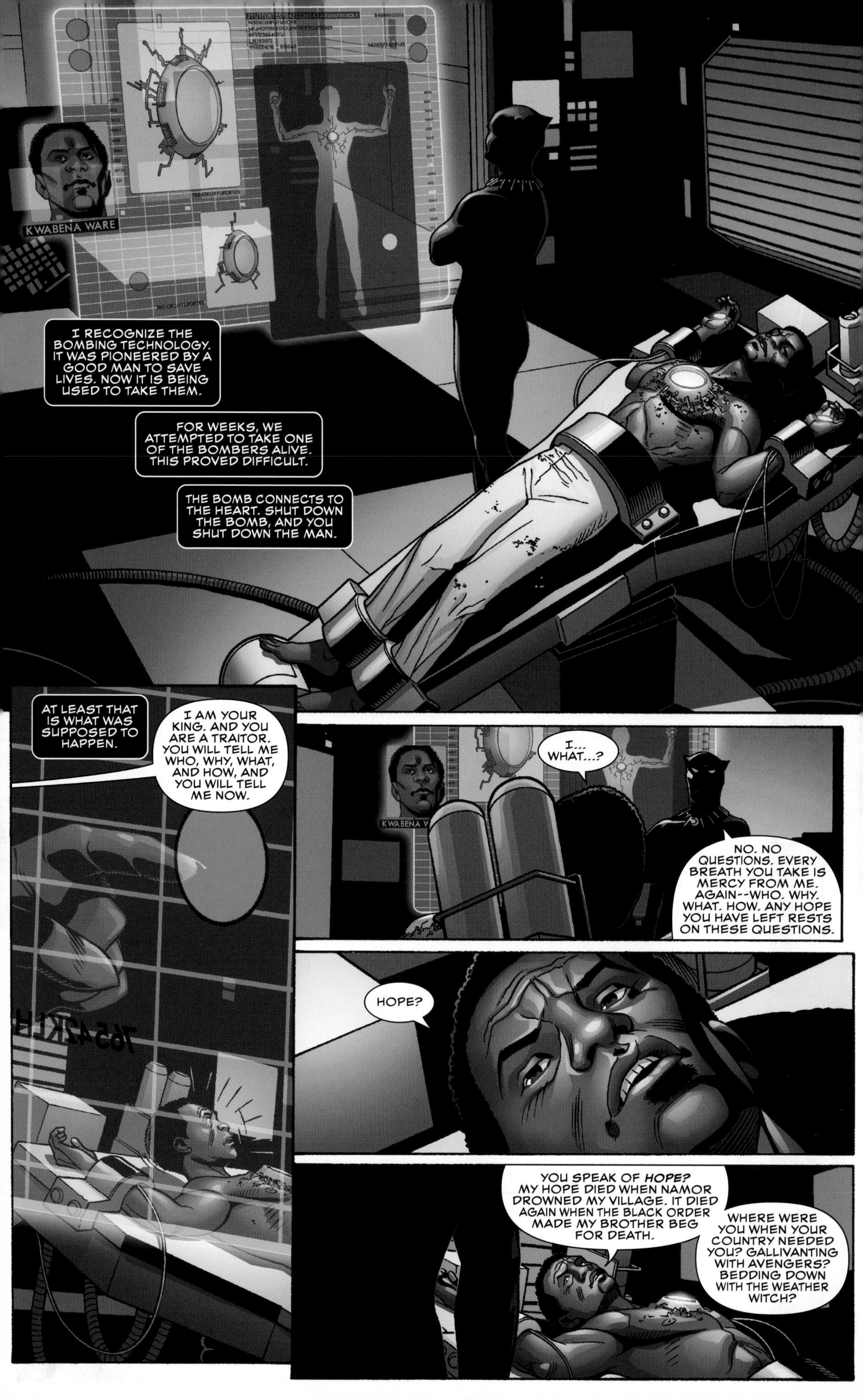
KWABENA WARE
I RECOGNIZE THE BOMBING TECHNOLOGY. IT WAS PIONEERED BY A GOOD MAN TO SAVE LIVES. NOW IT IS BEING USED TO TAKE THEM.
FOR WEEKS, WE ATTEMPTED TO TAKE ONE OF THE BOMBERS ALIVE. THIS PROVED DIFFICULT.
THE BOMB CONNECTS TO THE HEART. SHUT DOWN THE BOMB, AND YOU SHUT DOWN THE MAN.
AT LEAST THAT IS WHAT WAS SUPPOSED TO HAPPEN.
I AM YOUR KING. AND YOU ARE A TRAITOR. YOU WILL TELL ME WHO, WHY, WHAT, AND HOW, AND YOU WILL TELL ME NOW.
I... WHAT...?
NO. NO QUESTIONS. EVERY BREATH YOU TAKE IS MERCY FROM ME. AGAIN--WHO. WHY. WHAT. HOW. ANY HOPE YOU HAVE LEFT RESTS ON THESE QUESTIONS.
HOPE?
YOU SPEAK OF *HOPE?* MY HOPE DIED WHEN NAMOR DROWNED MY VILLAGE. IT DIED AGAIN WHEN THE BLACK ORDER MADE MY BROTHER BEG FOR DEATH.
WHERE WERE YOU WHEN YOUR COUNTRY NEEDED YOU? GALLIVANTING WITH AVENGERS? BEDDING DOWN WITH THE WEATHER WITCH?

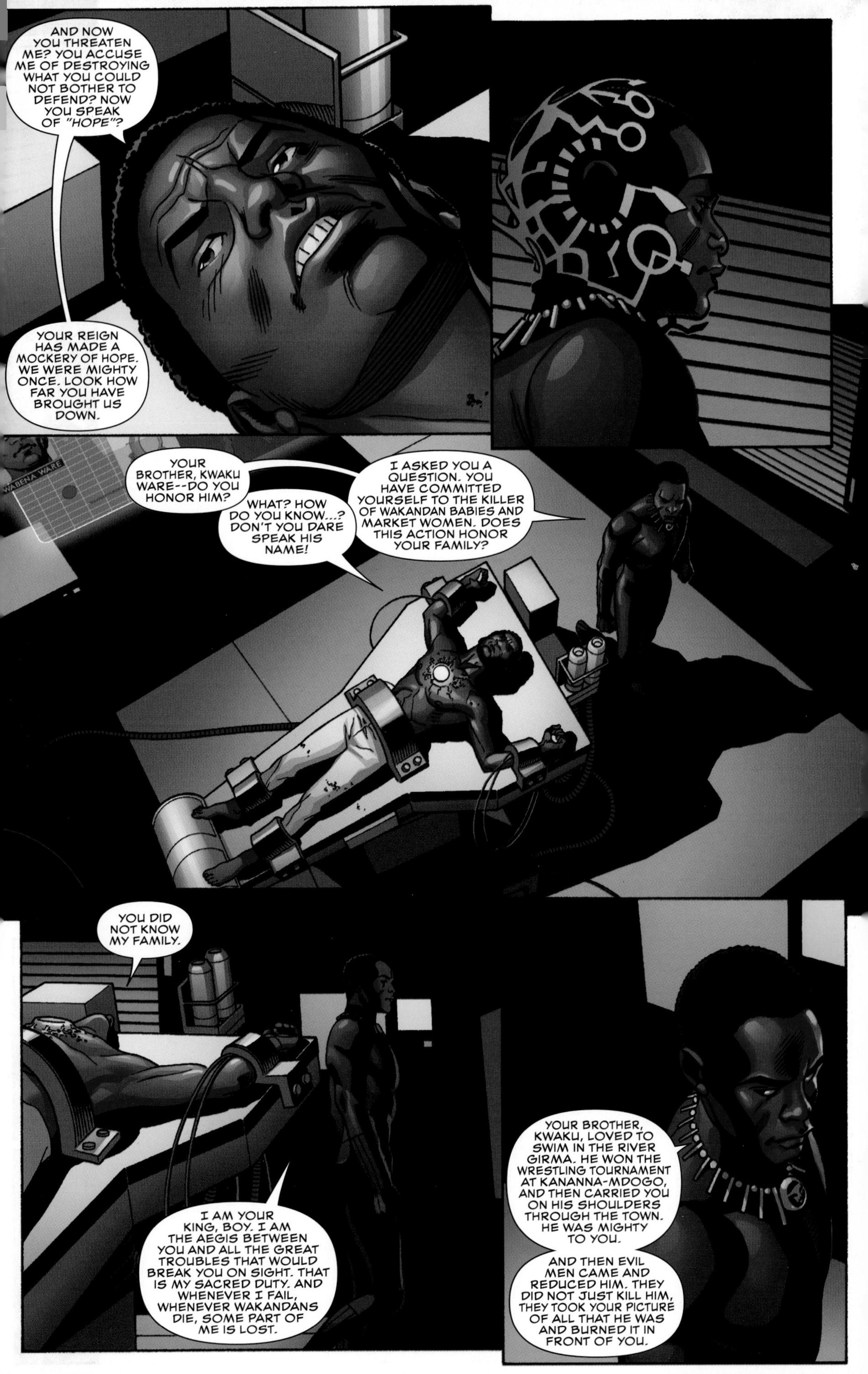
AND NOW YOU THREATEN ME? YOU ACCUSE ME OF DESTROYING WHAT YOU COULD NOT BOTHER TO DEFEND? NOW YOU SPEAK OF "HOPE"?
YOUR REIGN HAS MADE A MOCKERY OF HOPE. WE WERE MIGHTY ONCE. LOOK HOW FAR YOU HAVE BROUGHT US DOWN.
WABENA WARE
YOUR BROTHER, KWAKU WARE--DO YOU HONOR HIM?
WHAT? HOW DO YOU KNOW...? DON'T YOU DARE SPEAK HIS NAME!
I ASKED YOU A QUESTION. YOU HAVE COMMITTED YOURSELF TO THE KILLER OF WAKANDAN BABIES AND MARKET WOMEN. DOES THIS ACTION HONOR YOUR FAMILY?
YOU DID NOT KNOW MY FAMILY.
I AM YOUR KING, BOY. I AM THE AEGIS BETWEEN YOU AND ALL THE GREAT TROUBLES THAT WOULD BREAK YOU ON SIGHT. THAT IS MY SACRED DUTY. AND WHENEVER I FAIL, WHENEVER WAKANDANS DIE, SOME PART OF ME IS LOST.
YOUR BROTHER, KWAKU, LOVED TO SWIM IN THE RIVER GIRMA. HE WON THE WRESTLING TOURNAMENT AT KANANNA-MDOGO, AND THEN CARRIED YOU ON HIS SHOULDERS THROUGH THE TOWN. HE WAS MIGHTY TO YOU.
AND THEN EVIL MEN CAME AND REDUCED HIM. THEY DID NOT JUST KILL HIM, THEY TOOK YOUR PICTURE OF ALL THAT HE WAS AND BURNED IT IN FRONT OF YOU.

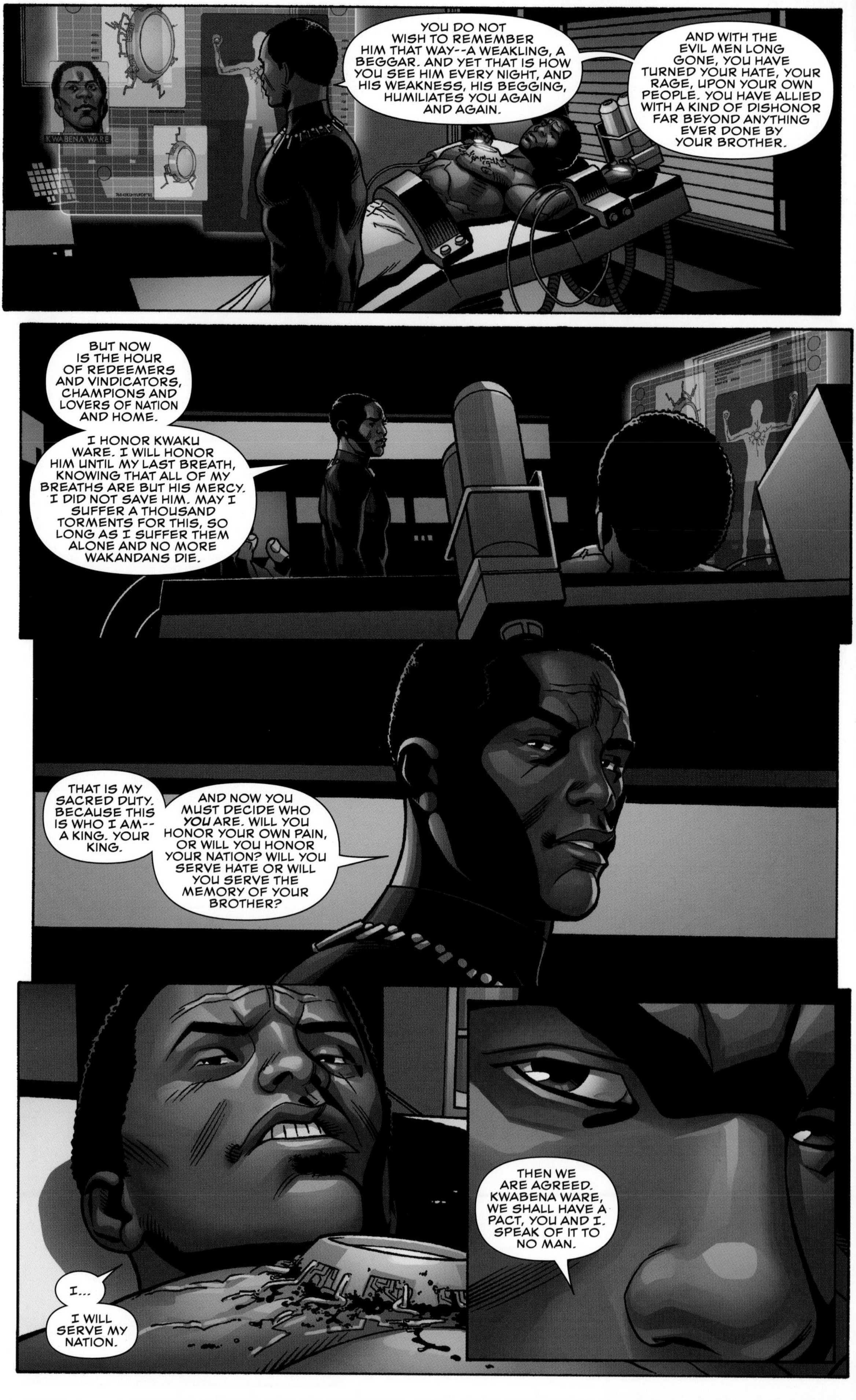
KWABENA WARE
YOU DO NOT WISH TO REMEMBER HIM THAT WAY--A WEAKLING, A BEGGAR. AND YET THAT IS HOW YOU SEE HIM EVERY NIGHT, AND HIS WEAKNESS, HIS BEGGING, HUMILIATES YOU AGAIN AND AGAIN.
AND WITH THE EVIL MEN LONG GONE, YOU HAVE TURNED YOUR HATE, YOUR RAGE, UPON YOUR OWN PEOPLE. YOU HAVE ALLIED WITH A KIND OF DISHONOR FAR BEYOND ANYTHING EVER DONE BY YOUR BROTHER.
BUT NOW IS THE HOUR OF REDEEMERS AND VINDICATORS, CHAMPIONS AND LOVERS OF NATION AND HOME.
I HONOR KWAKU WARE. I WILL HONOR HIM UNTIL MY LAST BREATH, KNOWING THAT ALL OF MY BREATHS ARE BUT HIS MERCY. I DID NOT SAVE HIM. MAY I SUFFER A THOUSAND TORMENTS FOR THIS, SO LONG AS I SUFFER THEM ALONE AND NO MORE WAKANDANS DIE.
THAT IS MY SACRED DUTY. BECAUSE THIS IS WHO I AM--A KING. YOUR KING.
AND NOW YOU MUST DECIDE WHO *YOU* ARE. WILL YOU HONOR YOUR OWN PAIN, OR WILL YOU HONOR YOUR NATION? WILL YOU SERVE HATE OR WILL YOU SERVE THE MEMORY OF YOUR BROTHER?
I...
I WILL SERVE MY NATION.
THEN WE ARE AGREED. KWABENA WARE, WE SHALL HAVE A PACT, YOU AND I. SPEAK OF IT TO NO MAN.

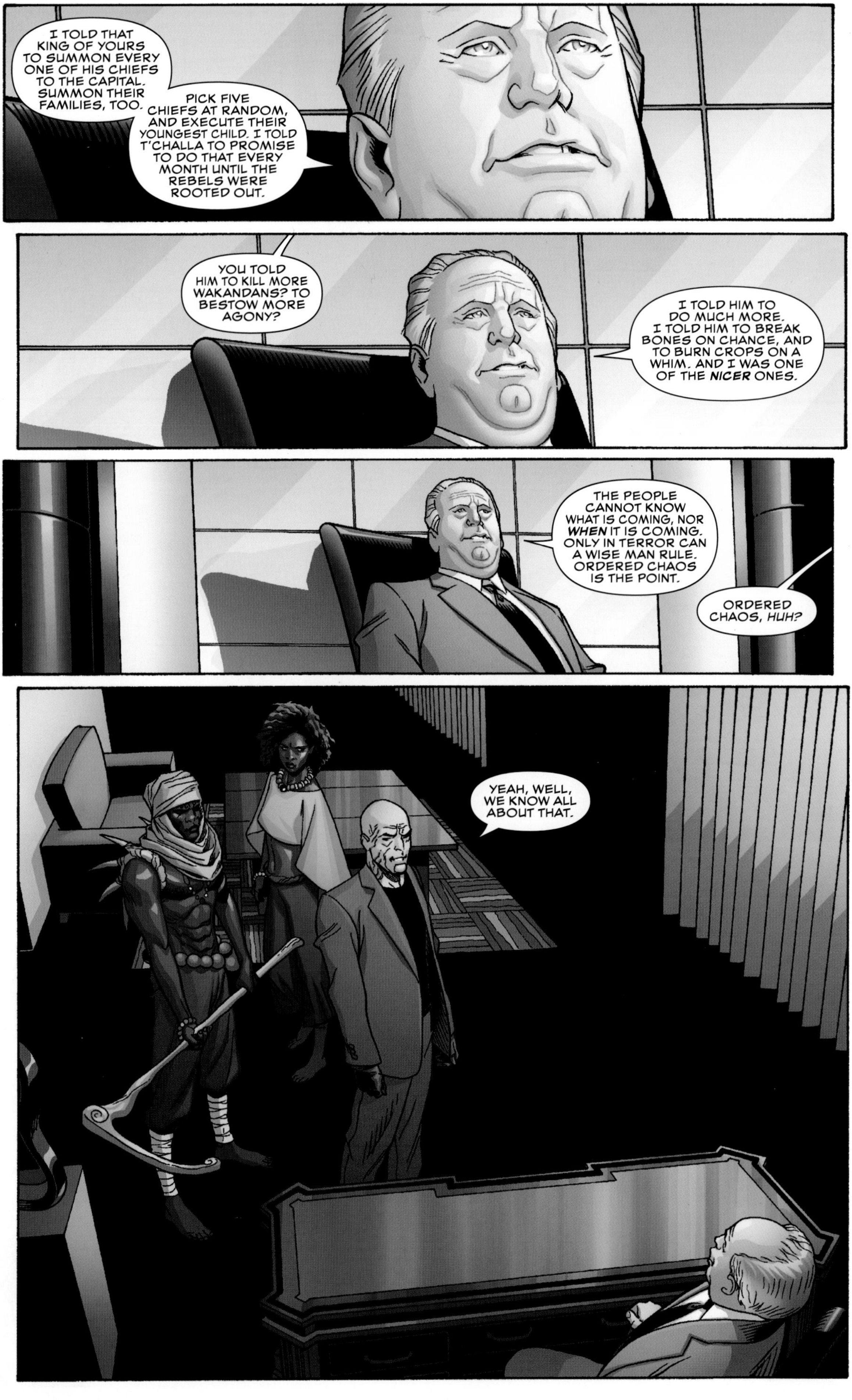
I TOLD THAT KING OF YOURS TO SUMMON EVERY ONE OF HIS CHIEFS TO THE CAPITAL. SUMMON THEIR FAMILIES, TOO.
PICK FIVE CHIEFS AT RANDOM, AND EXECUTE THEIR YOUNGEST CHILD. I TOLD T'CHALLA TO PROMISE TO DO THAT EVERY MONTH UNTIL THE REBELS WERE ROOTED OUT.
YOU TOLD HIM TO KILL MORE WAKANDANS? TO BESTOW MORE AGONY?
I TOLD HIM TO DO MUCH MORE. I TOLD HIM TO BREAK BONES ON CHANCE, AND TO BURN CROPS ON A WHIM. AND I WAS ONE OF THE NICER ONES.
THE PEOPLE CANNOT KNOW WHAT IS COMING, NOR WHEN IT IS COMING. ONLY IN TERROR CAN A WISE MAN RULE. ORDERED CHAOS IS THE POINT.
ORDERED CHAOS, HUH?
YEAH, WELL, WE KNOW ALL ABOUT THAT.

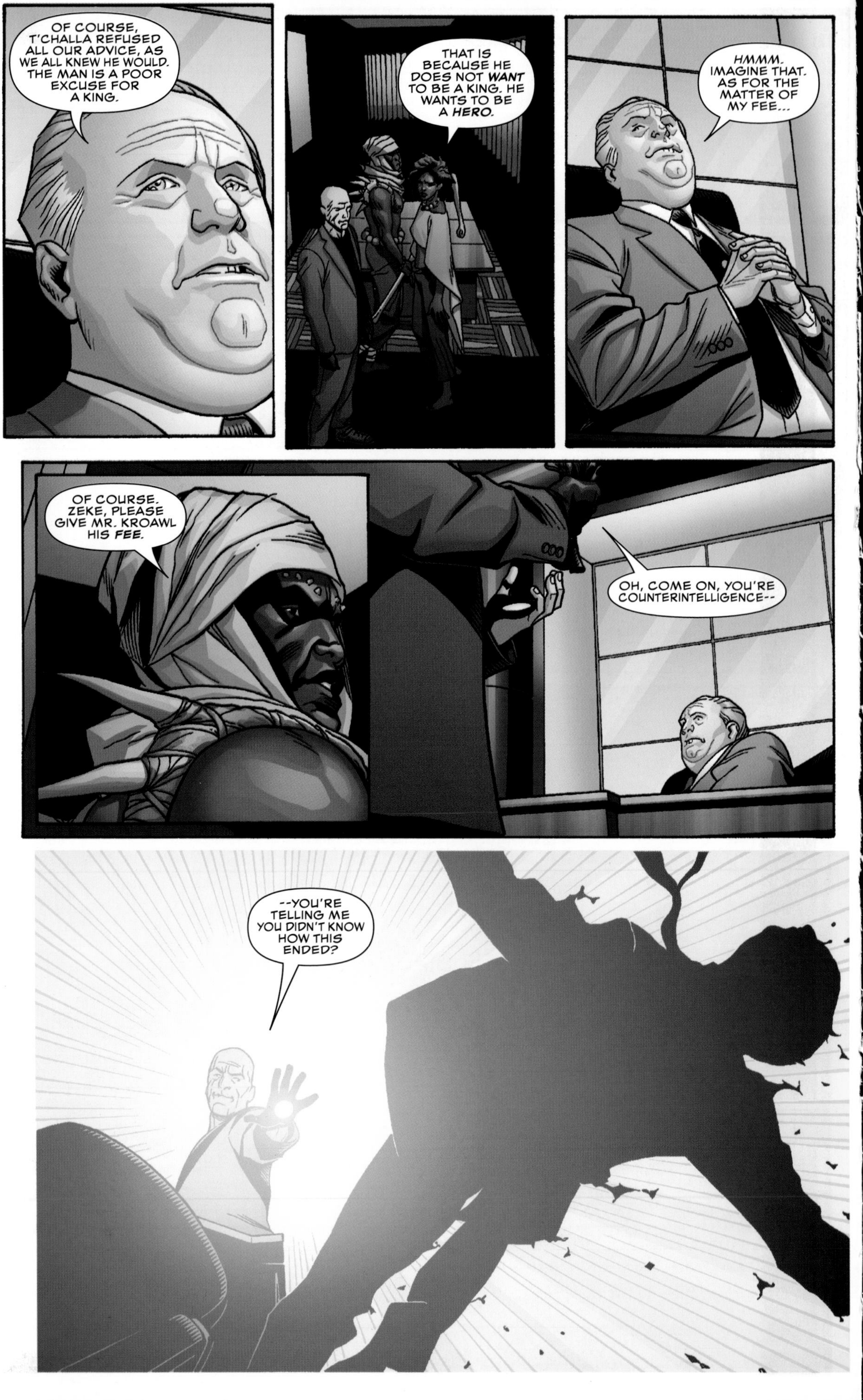
OF COURSE, T'CHALLA REFUSED ALL OUR ADVICE, AS WE ALL KNEW HE WOULD. THE MAN IS A POOR EXCUSE FOR A KING.
THAT IS BECAUSE HE DOES NOT WANT TO BE A KING. HE WANTS TO BE A HERO.
HMMM. IMAGINE THAT. AS FOR THE MATTER OF MY FEE...
OF COURSE. ZEKE, PLEASE GIVE MR. KROAWL HIS FEE.
OH, COME ON, YOU'RE COUNTERINTELLIGENCE--
--YOU'RE TELLING ME YOU DIDN'T KNOW HOW THIS ENDED?

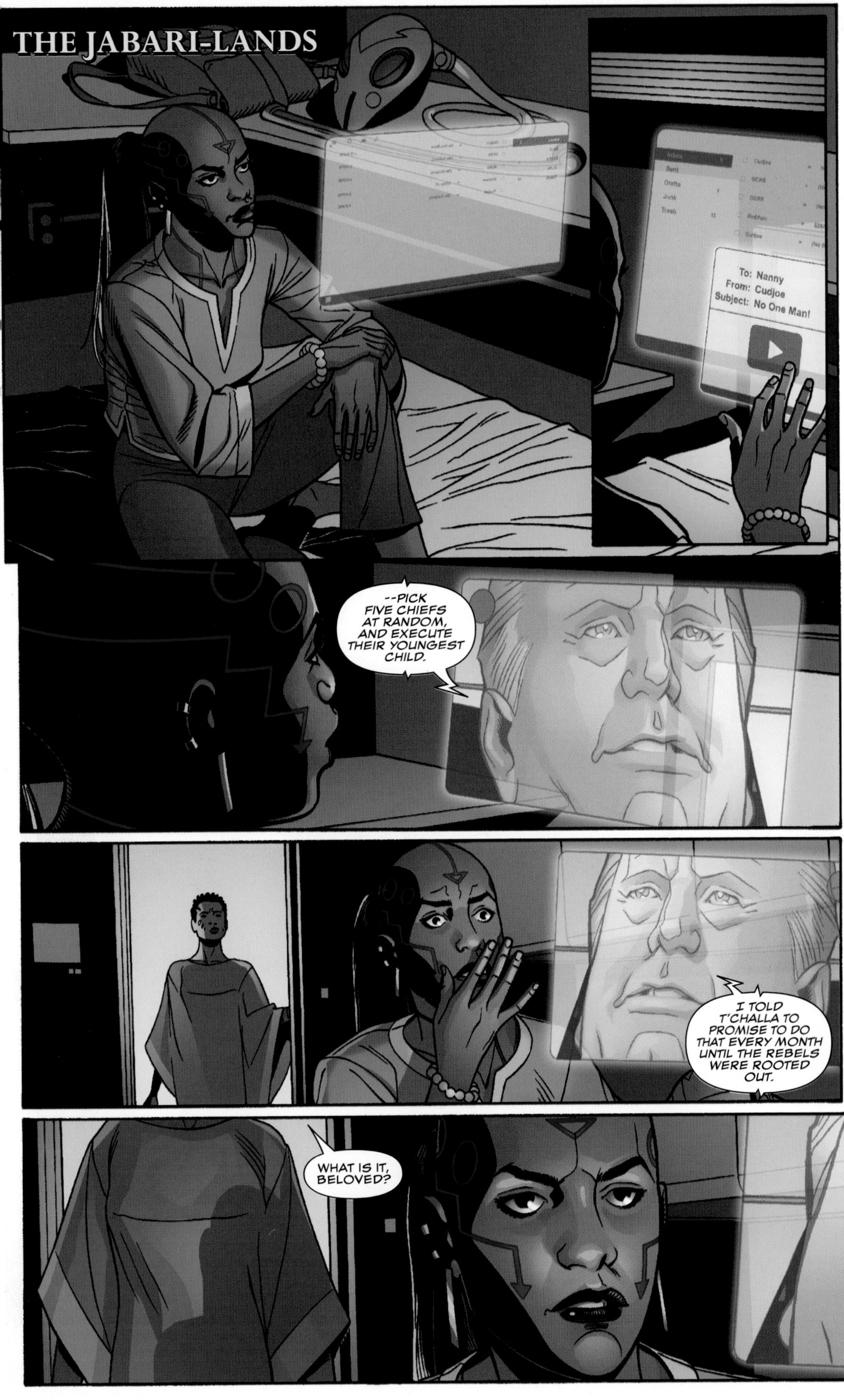
THE JABARI-LANDS
To: Nanny
From: Cudjoe
Subject: No One Man!
--PICK FIVE CHIEFS AT RANDOM, AND EXECUTE THEIR YOUNGEST CHILD.
I TOLD T'CHALLA TO PROMISE TO DO THAT EVERY MONTH UNTIL THE REBELS WERE ROOTED OUT.
WHAT IS IT, BELOVED?

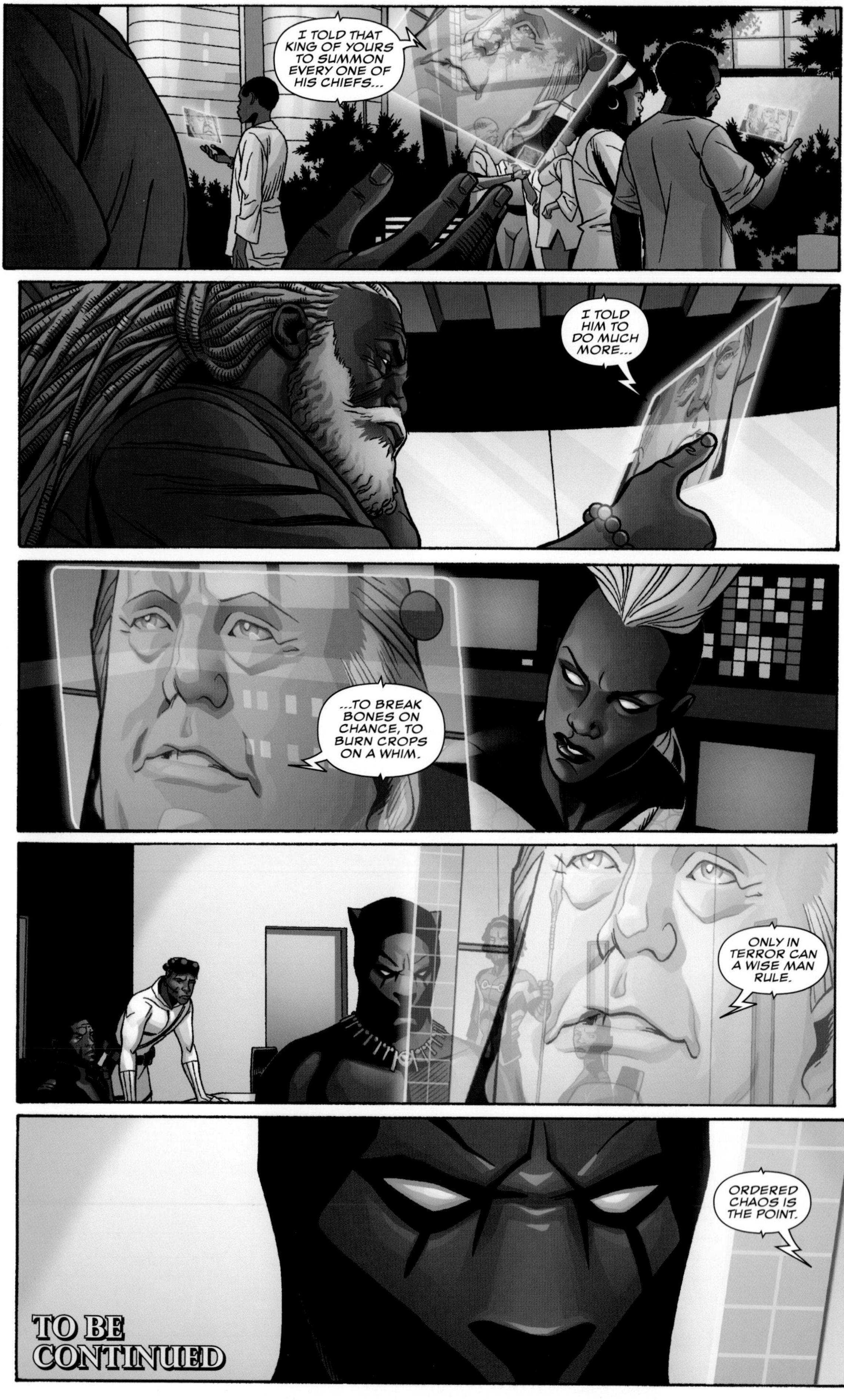
I TOLD THAT KING OF YOURS TO SUMMON EVERY ONE OF HIS CHIEFS...
I TOLD HIM TO DO MUCH MORE...
...TO BREAK BONES ON CHANCE, TO BURN CROPS ON A WHIM.
ONLY IN TERROR CAN A WISE MAN RULE.
ORDERED CHAOS IS THE POINT.
TO BE CONTINUED